Fred AND Ted's
Treasure Hunt

Hilda Offen

HUTCHINSON

LONDON SYDNEY AUCKLAND JOHANNESBURG

Here's a map in a bottle.

What does it say?

Row to the island out in the bay.

(And how many fish can you count on the way?)

Take eight steps forward

and five back again.

Whirl round and round

while you count up to ten.

Now – seven steps sideways!
Look up in the tree.

How many monkeys?

One!   Two!   Three!

1   2   3

(The monkeys say
please go that way.)

So – six jumps forward!
Now five! Now three!

And follow the turtles
down to the sea.

How many seashells
on the seashore?

Count on your fingers –
the answer is FOUR!

Shells whisper secrets;
take one in your hand.

How many spades can
you see in the sand?

Are you ready? Get steady!
Dig nine spadefuls each.

A chest full of treasure
lies under the beach.

Turn the key in the lock –
click-clackety-clack!

Seven twists forward,
another five back.

Whoosh! There goes a rabbit!
And there goes a bear!
Toy after toy shoots up
in the air.

How many rabbits?
And how many cats?
And how many teddies
in red woolly hats?

TREASURE MAP

Look up!

5 steps back

7 steps sideways

whirl round

8 steps forward

Land here

For Thomas Michael Goodyer

First published in 1999

1 3 5 7 9 10 8 6 4 2

First published in the United Kingdom in 1999 by
Hutchinson Children's Books
Random House UK Limited
20 Vauxhall Bridge Road, London SW1V 2SA

Random House Australia (Pty) Limited
20 Alfred Street, Milsons Point, Sydney
New South Wales 2061, Australia

Random House New Zealand Limited
18 Poland Road, Glenfield
Auckland 10, New Zealand

Random House South Africa (Pty) Limited
Endulini, 5A Jubilee Road, Parktown 2193, South Africa

Random House UK Limited Reg. No. 954009

A CIP catalogue record for this book is
available from the British Library

ISBN 0 09 176803 9

Printed in China